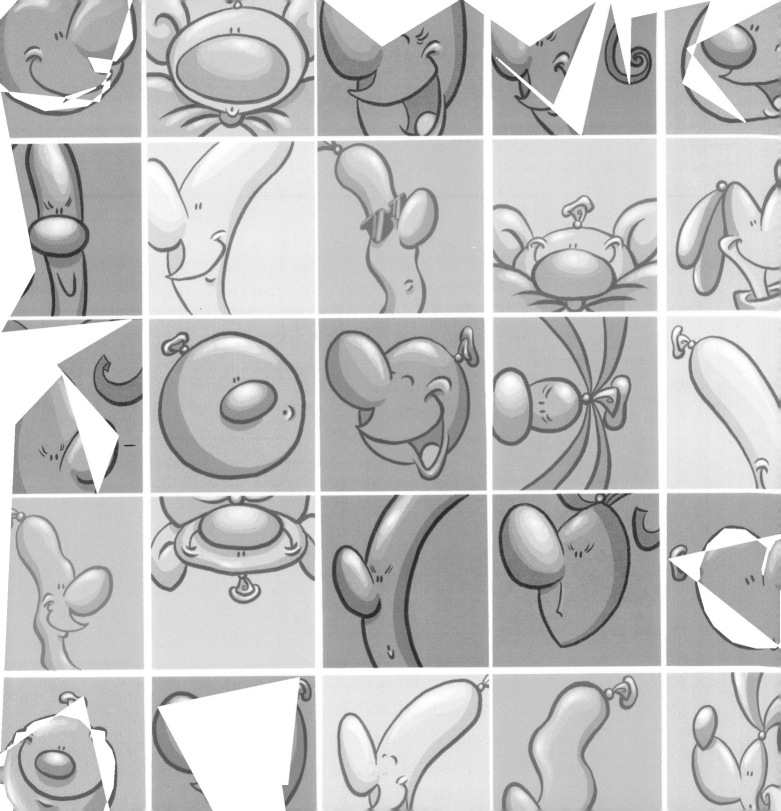

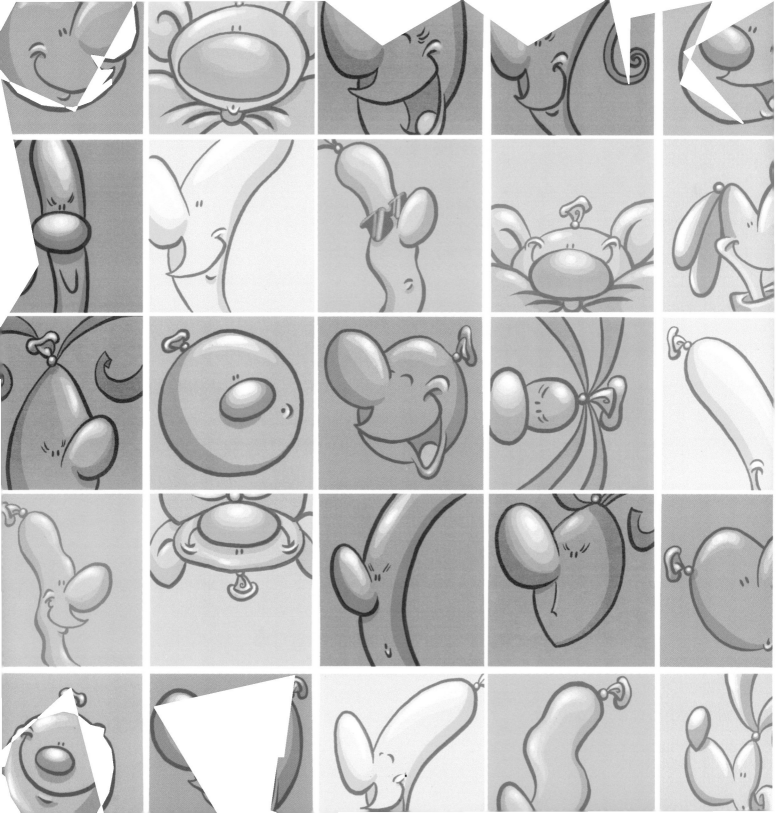

The BOSTON BALLOONIES

ISBN 978-1-933212-66-1

Designed by John Barnett/4 Eyes Design

Commonwealth Editions
an imprint of Applewood Books
P.O. Box 27, Carlisle, Massachusetts 01741
Visit us on the web at www.commonwealtheditions.com.

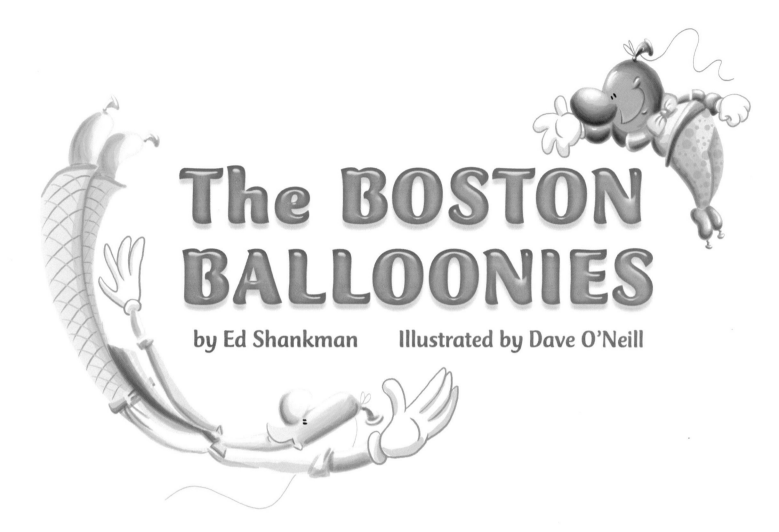

The BOSTON BALLOONIES

by Ed Shankman   Illustrated by Dave O'Neill

Commonwealth Editions
Carlisle, Massachusetts

The Boston Balloonies
Float all over town.
They whirl and they twirl
And they bounce up and down.

With a whee and a whoosh,
And a swoop and a swish,
They go swooping and swishing
Wherever they wish.

They drift down the alleys.
They glide up the streets.
They float past the shops
That sell silver and sweets.

And the ones that sell books,
And a few that sell jeans,
And a bunch that are known
For their Boston Baked Beans!

From Charles Street to Chestnut,
From Tremont to Mass,
The Balloonies sail on,
And they wave as they pass.

They wave to the kids
On the Swan Boats and trolleys.
They wave to the Billys
And Heathers and Hollys.

They pass by South Station,
And through Copley Square,
Where they share a few words
With the tortoise and hare.

They know every corner.
They go everywhere.
And a butler on Beacon Hill
Saw them up there!

Yes, they do get around,
There's no question they do,
But the Boston Balloonies
Do other things too.

For example, they're quite
Fond of music, you know,
And they're never too busy
To put on a show.

They play banjos and bongos
And oboes and flutes,
And the one who plays trumpet
Swells up when he toots.

There's a beautiful singer
Who hollers and hoots,
And some back-up Balloonies
With fabulous boots.

I know what you're thinking:
That's too good to miss.
But that's only half of it—
Listen to this!

The Balloonies showed up
At the Common one day
And presented a Boston
Balloony ballet.

Most people say
It was quite a display.
And then the Balloonies
Flew off on their way.

They breezed into Fenway
To take in a game.
And I tell you they knew
Every player by name.

They marked all their scorecards
And sat in their box,
Munching on hot dogs
And cheering the Sox.

They watched every inning,
And when they were through, . . .

...they whirled and they twirled
To the Franklin Park Zoo.

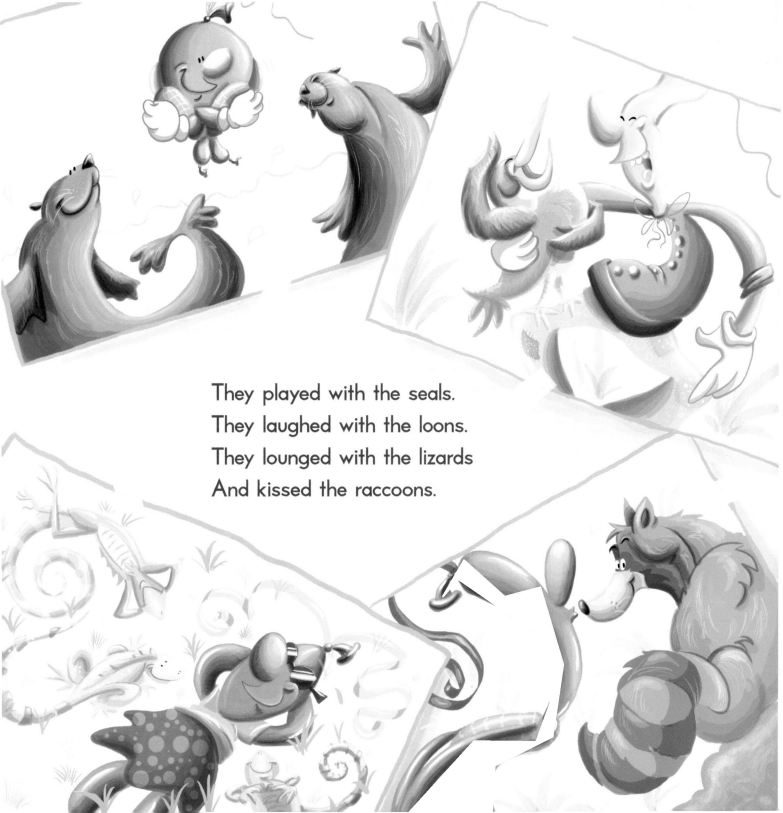

They played with the seals.
They laughed with the loons.
They lounged with the lizards
And kissed the raccoons.

And then, just like magic,
They took on the shape
Of the camel, the hippo,
The snake, and the ape!

Franklin Park **ZOO**

And we all tipped our hats
Because, son of a gun,
Those loony Balloonies
Know how to have fun!

And the fun wasn't through
When they flew from the zoo.
They had *more* games to play.
There was much more to do.

The Balloonies were ready
To try something new.
And that's when the Charles River
Came into view!

So they jumped in the water
And went for a ride.
They simply decided
To glide with the tide.

And they had no need
For a raft or a boat,
Because, as you know,
The Balloonies can float!

They can float on their sides.
They can float on their backs.
They can float just for fun.
They can float to relax.

They can float playing ping-pong,
Or checkers, or jacks.
I know it's amazing,
But those are the facts!

Balloonies can float
And Balloonies can fly.
And I mean they can fly
Really high in the sky.

They might go as high
As a bird or a bat,
And I've heard they can go
Even higher than that!

At night the Balloonies
Drift down to the park,
And they put on pajamas
That glow in the dark.

Then they tie a big bow
To a bench down below,
And they rise to the skies
Where they drift to and fro.

The Boston Balloonies
Have very sweet dreams.
'Cause they dream that their life
Is as good as it seems.

They know that the morning
Is coming, and then,
They'll go floating and twirling
And bouncing again.

In Boston you must
Watch the people you meet.
You just never know
Who may float down the street.

If they whirl and they twirl,
And their colors are bright,
You may guess who they are, . . .

...And, my friend, you'll be right!

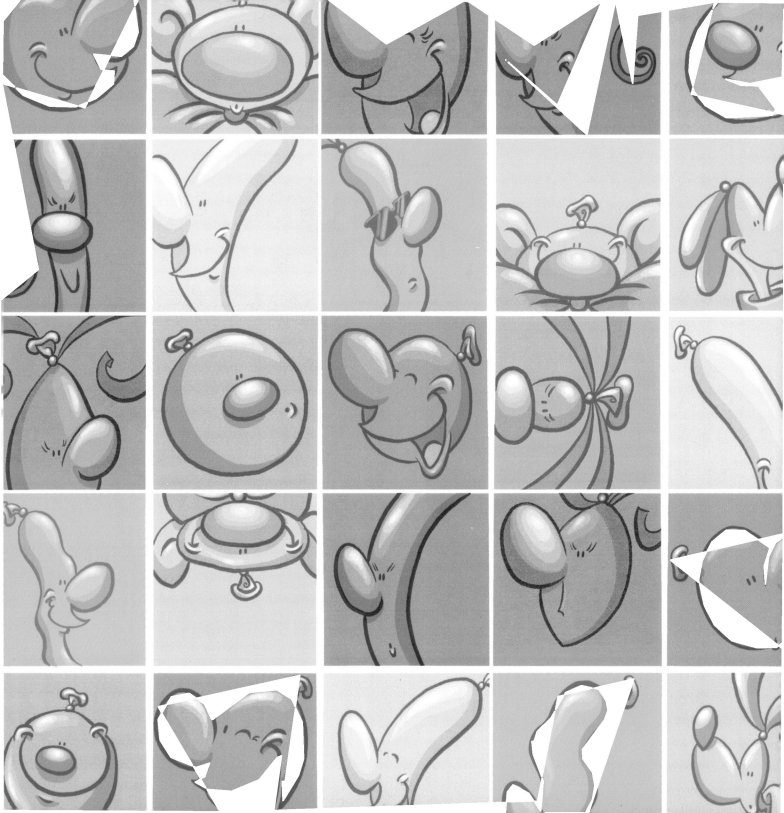

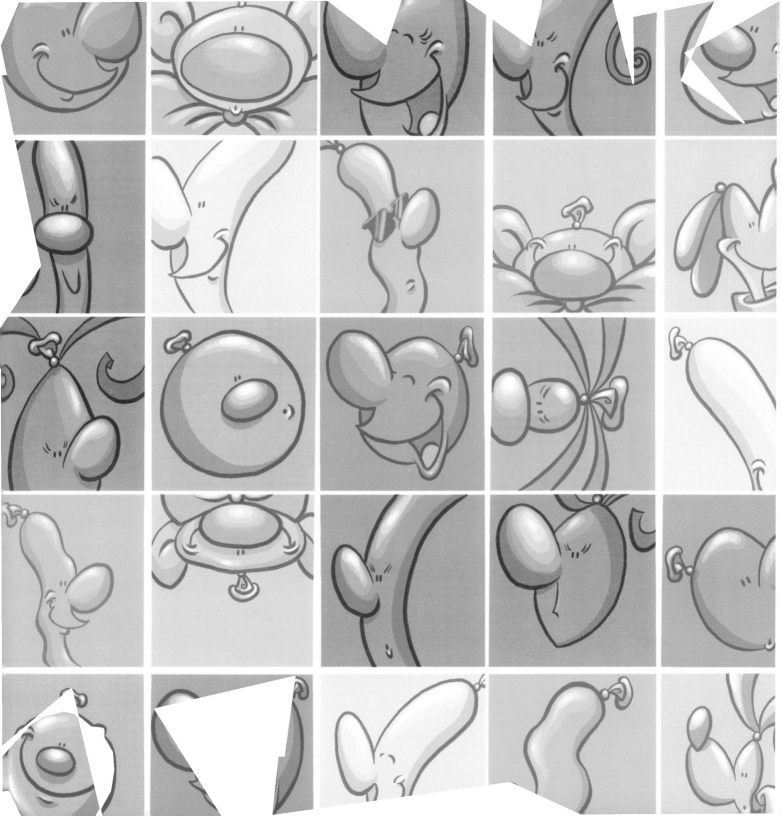

CPSIA information can be obtained
at www.ICGtesting.com
Printed in the USA
LVIW021448010313

322333LV00002B